Dinosaur with an Attitude

Hanna Johansen

Dinosaur
with an Attitude

Translation by Elisabetta Maccari

With linoleum print illustrations
by Hanna Johansen

Wetlands Press A DIVISION OF RDR BOOKS
Berkeley, California

First Wetlands Press Edition March 1994

Published in the United States of America
by Wetlands Press, a division of RDR Books. First
published in Switzerland as *Dinosaurier gibt es nicht*
by Nagel & Kimche, Zurich, 1992.

ISBN 1-57143-018-0

Library of Congress Catalog Card Number: 94-60000

American Edition Editor: Wendy Ann Logsdon

The American publisher acknowledges the generous
assistance of Renate Nagel, Bonnie Smetts, Sven
Niemetz, Deborah Dunn, Calvin Goodman, Richard
Harris, Heika Abeck and Li Suk Woon.

Wetlands Press, a division of RDR Books, P.O. Box
5212, Berkeley, CA 94705

Printed in China by Twin Age Limited.

About the Author

Hanna Johansen-Muschg was born in 1939 in Bremen,
Germany. She studied German, Classical Linguistics, and
Education in Marburg and Gottingen. Today she lives with
her two children in Klichberg, near Zurich. The stories she
originally created for her own children became her first
children's books. She received the 1984 Hans Christian
Anderson Award, and her latest book, Dinosaur with an
Attitude, won the German Academy's Book of the Month
Award for children's literature in December 1992, as well as
the 1993 Austrian Children's Book Prize. Her children's
books have been translated into 13 languages.

CONTENTS

THE NEW NAME

My name is Zawinul now. I inherited the name, but not from my parents. I inherited it from a friend, because Zawinul is a name that has to be passed on. He put up with the name for a couple of years. Then he had enough of it. Why? Nothing but trouble, that's what he said. But that was later. In the beginning, my friend was enthusiastic. Because as long as he was called Zawinul, every day he experienced something that was not normally possible. Before that his life had been too slow, too orderly, and above all, too boring.

After he inherited the name everything went much faster. Tedious tasks almost took care of themselves. Holidays he used to wait for came immediately. Summer took a bit longer to arrive, but not as long as before. Boredom no longer existed.

"Omps!"

And we haven't spoken about the most important part yet. All sorts of things which were impossible actually became possible as soon as Zawinul was near. And when he told his stories, they sounded so improbable that no one wanted to believe him. But they had happened to him. His friends didn't hold it against him. But when they heard about his experiences, they simply said, "Nonsense."

"Omps!"

"Omps?" I said to myself. "Who's saying 'Omps'?"

"Omps!"

"Quiet!" I said, because the ompsing was bothering me. But there was no one there, and when there's no one there, no one can stop ompsing either.

Only a day had passed since my friend had asked me if I wanted to have his name. I was really crazy about being called Zawinul. And my friend Zawinul was crazy about giving me his name. He jumped up in the air,

10

squeezed my hand and said, "Good luck, Zawinul."

And I was happy.

"Omps!"

I had never heard anyone say 'omps' before. Besides, there was a crackling sound. This should be expected when your name is Zawinul. You imagine all sorts of things.

"Omps!"

I had had too much to eat for lunch and the food didn't agree with me. But is that a reason to doubt my common sense? Maybe. I counted what was left of my Easter eggs: one, two, three. Very good. I was satisfied with myself, because if I could count to three, I hadn't lost my common sense. Of course, you couldn't eat the eggs anymore. They were sitting on the window sill between the cactus and the asparagus fern. The potted palm hovered over them. The three eggs lay in a green nest padded with green straw. One was decorated with gold-fish, the other with pale blue Easter bunnies. The third egg was the one I liked best. It had ferns and plants painted on it, and from behind these plants a small animal peered forth. The animal looked like an unusual lizard, but I could see what it was meant to be. The lines were drawn so finely that they looked like cracks in the eggshell. To me it was a special egg. I had found it in the garden, under the daffodils.

But who, now, was saying "Omps"? I was home alone. Maybe it was me? Maybe I, Zawinul, was sitting at the window on a sunny afternoon, saying "Omps" without realizing it. That does happen, especially

when you've eaten too much.

"Omps!"

No, that wasn't me.

Who was it then? I looked under the table. I lay down flat on my stomach in order to check whether someone was hiding under the sofa saying "Omps." Of course, no one was there. Everyone knows that there's never anyone under the sofa. There was no one under the desk, either. And there definitely was nobody on top of the shelves. That was a little harder to find out. I had to get a chair and climb on the back. From up there I could see at a glance that no one was lying on the shelves. Then the chair broke down. I was unharmed, the chair wasn't. Carefully, I dragged the pieces into the next room and hid them under the bed. You can forget about things that are under the bed for a while.

All afternoon I was home alone. I stood by the second-floor window and listened. The house was full of sounds: rustling, clinking, rattling, doors slamming, voices, music, rumbling and ringing. I also heard barking, screeching, and whistling. I heard lots of other noises that belong to this house. But a voice that very softly says "Omps" did not belong.

"Omps!"

Besides, there was the crackling sound. In fact, it was one of my three eggs that was crackling like that. It was also this egg that was saying "Omps."

That can't be, I thought. Easter eggs don't crackle, and Easter eggs don't speak. Easter eggs are stone-dead, because they're boiled. Perhaps the egg wasn't boiled after all? For a couple of weeks, it had been lying in the hot April sun that shone in through the window. Maybe the sun had hatched out a little chicken and it was now trying to get out of its shell? That happens, but not with chickens.

"Zawinul," I said to myself, in order to get

14

accustomed to the new name. "Zawinul, that's a pretty dumb idea."

The egg was smaller than the others. It didn't have the same shape, either. It was flatter and longer. And then I saw cracks opening up between the painted ferns, becoming longer and larger, until finally the egg burst open. A head peered out. His look was a bit glassy. He had black eyes and a very thin neck. This was not a chicken; I could tell that right away.

I said, "Zawinul, what kind of a bird is this, if it's not a chicken?"

The animal was a pretty peculiar bird, because it didn't have any feathers. Nor did it have hair or bristles. It was totally naked. I stood at the window, stared at the clouds and thought for a while. Then I stared at the animal again, shook my head, and whispered, "Zawinul, what you are seeing here does not exist."

"Omps," whispered the animal.

This wasn't a chicken, it wasn't even a bird. Its face was full of wrinkles. It resembled a lizard, in a way. But in a way it didn't. Lizards don't come out of such big eggs. It also resembled a crocodile. But crocodiles don't come out of such small eggs.

I had a hunch. I'd rather not talk about it. After all, it was only a hunch.

The animal placed something like tiny little hands on the edge of the eggshell and pulled itself up. It turned its black eyes to the left, to the right, upwards, looked down over the edge of the eggshell, then nodded with relief and said, "Comps!!!"

A Peculiar Chick

 The truth has to come out sometime. My suspicion was right. What had worked its way out of my Easter egg there on my window sill was not a bird. It wasn't a lizard and it wasn't a snake. It wasn't even a crocodile. I was glad about that, because crocodiles bite. It could only be a dinosaur. He was now looking at me very attentively. Once more, he whispered, "Comps!" Then he laid his head on the edge of the eggshell in order to rest. His eyes closed.

Until now I had only seen his top half. But there was no doubt about it. I hadn't read all those books about dinosaurs for nothing. He had no spikes, no horns, no crest, no large armor plates, he had only wrinkles. He probably didn't even have teeth, but I couldn't see that while he was hanging over the edge of his eggshell, completely exhausted with his eyes closed. I watched him sleeping. A beauty he wasn't. Nonetheless, I liked him at first sight. That probably had nothing to do with his being a dinosaur. It was because he was so small. All babies are cute, at least in the beginning.

He wasn't half the size of my hand.

"Zawinul," I said, "don't get carried away. They grow."

I didn't know whether to laugh or to cry. We all know what happens with dinosaurs once they're out of the egg. The question was how fast they grew. And how long they grew.

I got up quietly to get my books. What I found out was the following: They grow very

fast in the beginning, more and more slowly with time, but never stop completely until the very end. Some dinosaurs grow to be thirty meters long, any child knows that. But no one knows if they then weigh as much as twelve elephants or only as much as three elephants. To me, at this moment, it made no difference whether they weighed eighty or fifteen tons. For me, a single ton was already too much if it was going to settle on my window sill.

There were also dinosaurs that didn't even grow half that big. When they stood up, they were only as tall as a two-story house. Then again, they were ten times as dangerous as the big ones.

Skeptically, I looked at the tiny animal under the potted palm. It sighed in its sleep and whispered:

"An elephant eats eighty pounds of fresh feed each day." I could not imagine an eighty pound pile. Nor could I imagine what an animal weighing as much as a whole herd of elephants would eat.

"Zawinul," I said, "are you sure you like this?"

"O?" said the voice.

The strange chick had woken up again, it raised its head and began right away to climb over the edge of the eggshell. It fell down into the nest and lay there in the green straw. Then it continued to climb down until it was sitting on the window sill, between the cactus and the asparagus fern. Without a doubt this was a dinosaur, although it was a small one. Its hind part was exactly as I had expected: a long tail and two strong little legs that looked like they would become much longer and stronger. His arms, in comparison, were quite tiny and had pretty little claws. Two, not more. "O?" he said again, looking inquiringly first at me and then at everything else.

A thought came to me that I didn't like at all. Maybe he was hungry? What now? How should I know what to do when a dinosaur

20

chick is hungry? Get grass? Nuts or rolled oats? Luckily, I knew that when chicks have worked their way out of their egg, they don't need something to eat right away. There was no hurry to cut dandelions. But perhaps dandelions weren't enough when hunger came. Maybe an animal like him needed duckweed or water lily blossoms? Or maybe flies? Did I have to hunt for worms, millipedes, and snails? And did I have to keep them in the refrigerator, right next to the lettuce and the cheese?

My dinosaur started walking around. Walking around is not the right word for his way of moving about. He tried it more or less with all four legs. This looked all wrong, because the front legs were much too short for walking. But without them it didn't work either, because the hind legs were much too wobbly. So he stumbled on. He wanted to see and smell everything. All the time it sounded like he was mumbling one word over and over again, "Gnathus...gnathus... gnathus..."

"Gnathus?"

He pulled himself up on the flower pots, in order to look inside. He could only do this with the small ones. When he reached the potted palm he craned his neck, tilted back his pointed head, looked upwards, and couldn't take his eyes off the many feather-like leaves.

"Gnathus!" he mumbled.

Gnathus? What was he trying to say?

"Zawinul," I said to myself, "you have to learn his language."

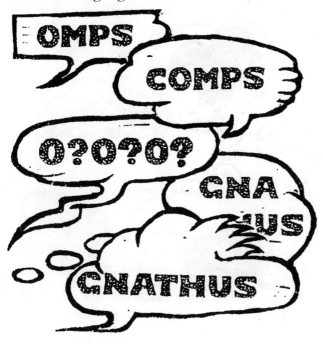

Until now I had only heard four words from him. He said "Omps" every time he had to do something difficult. He said "Comps" when he had managed to do it. He said "O?" in order to ask something and "Gnathus" for all the rest. Up to this point it wasn't difficult. The real difficulties began later.

I took my dinosaur, stuck him in the pocket of my jacket so that he couldn't mess

23

about with the flower pots, and went to the phone.

"I'll come right away," said my friend. This was the one who used to be called Zawinul and passed the name on to me. He always has time when I need him.

He took a thorough look at the animal.

"Zawinul," he said, shaking his head, "you must be out of your mind. Whatever this animal is, it can't be a dinosaur."

24

"And why not?"

"As far as I know, dinosaurs are a whole lot bigger."

"Even dinosaurs have to start off small," I said.

"Besides, dinosaurs are extinct."

"I've heard that too. But do you have to believe everything that's written in books? Maybe it's not true. Didn't books also claim for a long time that the earth was flat and that we could fall off the edges?"

He couldn't argue about that. But still he shook his head.

"And if today, one should hatch again," my friend finally said, "why, of all places, would he do it on the window sill of 140 Solnhofener Street, Zawinul?"

I could only laugh at that. Because when such an extraordinary event occurs, it can occur only on my window sill. After all, I'm called Zawinul now, and not him.

"And besides," I said, "what else can it be, if it's not a dinosaur, huh?"

I didn't think he would come up with anything. But he had more than one answer.

"A water lizard," he said. "An iguana, a small komodo dragon, a . . ."

"And how are they supposed to cross the oceans to get to Solnhofener Street?"

"With a ship, Zawinul."

"Let's just wait," I said. "We'll see what becomes of him."

TREMENDOUSLY BIG

 It was a beautiful day in May. The sun shone brightly through the window. I stared out gloomily and thought: Zawinul, it sure looks like you've got yourself a dinosaur now. That sounds alright, but to be honest, I would rather have had a chicken or a parrot, because you know how big they're going to get. Also, I started hearing that strange crackling sound on my window sill again.

"Not again," I said. "One dinosaur is enough."

Two eggs were still lying in the nest, one painted with a goldfish and the other with pale blue Easter bunnies. Hearing the crackling, I imagined the egg slowly cracking open from the inside and then a goldfish coming out of one and a blue rabbit out of the other.

I thought, that's impossible, Zawinul.

But isn't a dinosaur impossible too? That is the question. If dinosaurs are possible, goldfish and blue rabbits are possible too. Although, right now, they weren't possible because the crackling wasn't coming from the eggs at all. It came from my strange hatchling, who was walking around between the flower pots. It was already standing better on its hind legs and hardly needed its front feet any more. Maybe I was mistaken, I thought. Maybe you just have to give this animal time. Maybe it will turn into a bird after all. Maybe it will grow feathers when it's a little bigger. Maybe my friend is right about not believing in dinosaurs that hatch

out of Easter eggs. That is nonsense. Or rather, it would be nonsense, if he wasn't standing right here in front of me, large as life.

"Omps," said the dinosaur on my window sill. He was sniffing the plants standing there.

"Please don't eat them!" I said.

He wasn't interested in eating them. I was glad for the plants' sake. But as far as the dinosaur was concerned, I was less glad. If he didn't eat plants, he had to be a carnivore. Vegetarians are easier to feed. I tried grass, but he wouldn't touch it. He didn't eat lettuce, and he didn't eat apples. He didn't even eat the budding peonies.

He looked for stones in the cactus bowl. He picked out a couple of them, kept them in his mouth for a while and then swallowed them. Wonderful, I thought. Animals content with stones are easy to feed. But I had rejoiced too soon. He was not content with stones. They were just the hors d'œvre that made his hunger worse. I had to find something for him to eat, soon. And it had to be something alive.

"Zawinul," I said, "it's time to go fly-catching, worm-digging, and snail-hunting."

29

Luckily, I came up with something simpler. For a start, I tried cat food. I always had a couple of cans in the house, because every now and then a cat came to visit me. It would climb over the rooftops, jump onto my balcony, and meow until I gave it something to eat. I opened a can and put a few chunks of beef on a plate. My dinosaur ate them, looked at me and said, "Tastes good!"

I will make a long story short. My peculiar bird was hungry day and night. He ate and ate, but didn't grow any feathers. Instead he began to get bigger.

Growing is something wonderful. Although I don't have the slightest idea about how it happens. I don't know what I have to do to make my legs or arms longer. But I am able to let them grow, because otherwise my arms and legs wouldn't have become as long as they are today. My dinosaur chick could do it too. I watched him grow and thought to myself: Where will this lead?

Pictures of feet came to mind, which by themselves were as big as a man. I saw skeletons before me that reached from one end of a museum to the other. I had seen teeth as long as bread-knives and as sharp as daggers with curved blades and jagged edges. A lot of numbers went through my head: three, nine, fifteen, twenty-one, twenty-seven, thirty-five feet. Everyone knows how big dinosaurs can get. Right now, my dinosaur was still a loveable little animal. But I was worried.

"Don't get upset, Zawinul," I said, "we shall see what becomes of him."

He didn't seem to care. He sat very still and listened to the buzzing of a fly. It was making various attempts in various places to fly through the window pane into the open. My dinosaur jumped. And he didn't miss. He looked at the fly in his hands for a while. Then he stuck it in his mouth and bit it in two. To say he didn't have any teeth was nonsense. He had quite a lot of them and they were pretty sharp teeth. Luckily they were small.

Zawinul, I thought, every single fly will make him a little bit bigger. The question is, how big?

"Very big," said the dinosaur.

"And how big is very big?"

31

"Tremendously big," said the dinosaur.

I had been afraid of that. "How big is tremendously big?"

"About like this!" he said, stood up on his hind legs and stretched high. In this way he could already look over the edge of the pot of the potted palm. "That big!"

"Not any bigger?"

"Any bigger?" he said, looking at me skeptically. "Isn't that big enough?"

"Oh yes," I said with relief. "That's big enough."

But to be honest, I didn't believe him. What could such a small animal that had just hatched out of an egg know about dinosaurs? I couldn't rid myself of the suspicion that he would soon be as big as a Triceratops and then a Tyrannosaurus. Possibly, he wouldn't stop growing when he had reached the size of a Brachiosaurus, and ultimately become the size of a Supersaurus. And then what?

"Don't get upset, Zawinul," I said. "Look it up."

I put on my jacket.

"Where are you going?" my dinosaur squeaked.

"To the library," I said. "You stay here and lie down on your pillow." I had prepared a warm place for him in a basket. The basket stood next to my bed, so that he wouldn't feel lonely.

"Please don't squeak!" I said, because he was looking at me as if he didn't want to let me go.

He squeaked anyway.

Then I went to the library to take out more books. They had to be new. A short while ago maybe three hundred species of dinosaurs were known, or to be exact, two hundred and eighty-one with certainty and sixty-nine possibly. Now new ones were being found daily, because thousands of

33

paleontologists were busy with their shovels and brushes, digging up more bones of extinct animals. Under these circumstances, how was I going to identify my dinosaur? Maybe he belonged to a species that hadn't yet been discovered?

When I came home with the books, my neighbors opened their door to warn me they had heard strange noises coming from the kitchen. "Maybe something's broken," they said.

But nothing was broken in the kitchen. There were just pots lying on the floor. I put everything away again, sat down at the table, and opened the books in order to find out what kind of a dinosaur I had. It wasn't at all as hard as I thought. I had to leave aside most of the species right away. After all, he had neither spikes, nor horns, nor a crest, nor large armor plates. He just had wrinkles, which seemed to be smoothing out. I could forget about the herbivores too, because he still didn't feel like feeding on horsetail, fern fronds, palm ferns, or pine-needles. Some of the dinosaurs in the books had front legs that were too long, others had feet that were too large or had too many toes. But daspletosaurs, tarbosaurs, and tyrannosaurs with their two claws fit pretty well. The thought started my heart pounding.

"Don't get upset," I said once more. "Look closely."

Taking a closer look, daspletosaurs, tarbosaurs, and tyrannosaurs had necks that were too short and heads too large. The only species left was the Compsognathus: "A quick predator that moves on two legs. A chicken-sized dinosaur from the Solnhofen Limestone in Germany." That had to be him.

"Now I know your name," I said to my dinosaur. "Compsognathus!"

He laughed. "I could have told you that right away," said the Compsognathus. Then he asked me, "And what's your name?"

"Zawinul."

"Funny name. Are you sure that's your name?"

"Of course my name is Zawinul," I said. In truth though, I wasn't so sure. I was still unused to the name because it hadn't quite stuck to me the way old names usually do.

COMPSOGNATHUS LONGLEGS

The Compsognathus thought of food all day. "Are you quite sure, Zawinul, you're not dealing with a crocodile here?" I said to myself. "With legs like that?" Zawinul answered back.

"A species of crocodile that's still unknown?"

"One that hops?"

"Why not?"

"Zawinul," I said, "crocodiles crawl, that's why they're called crocodiles. Otherwise they'd be called hopsodiles."

My dinosaur had gotten into the habit of hopping alongside me. I couldn't take one step without him being there. When I tried

37

to go to another room alone, he would start crying. Sometimes he walked next to my right leg, sometimes next to my left leg. Sometimes he walked next to both my legs at the same time. Especially when I put my jacket on to go outside, he would run around my legs in such close circles that I couldn't move anymore. He tugged at my knee.

"Omps," said the Compsognathus.

"That's what I just wanted to say."

"I want to come along," he said.

"You can't."

"Why not?"

"Because you . . .

38

because people . . .because I . . .because sometimes..." I said.

"Because what?"

All I could think of were excuses. A long row of pretty dumb excuses.

"Don't make such a fuss about it, Zawinul," I said. "He can come along."

"Comps," said the Compsognathus.

We'll pretend that he's a dog, I thought, then he won't attract any attention. We would need a leash then, but where could I get one? Should I ring at the neighbors' doorbell? They had a dog, and maybe they'd be so kind as to lend me a leash. I picked up the Compsognathus, hid him under my jacket, and rang the doorbell. First we heard Baxter in the kitchen. Then the door opened.

"A leash?" said the man from next door. "For a dog? What kind of a dog? A young one? Is he house-trained yet? Where's he from? A female or a male? Baxter will be delighted about this. What? You're saying it's not a dog at all?"

The man stared at me in disbelief. I would do the same if someone wanted to borrow a leash and didn't even have a dog.

"Thank you very much," I stuttered.

"Forget about it. Sorry to have bothered you. Goodbye."

I tucked the Compsognathus tighter under my jacket and went down the stairs. Right around the corner was a pet shop. We went there to buy a leash.

"Can I help you?"

"I need a leash for my dinosaur here."

The saleswoman smiled at the animal.

"What's his name?" she asked.

"Compsognathus."

"*Compsognathus longipes?*"

"Right," I said.

She nodded and said, "A beautiful specimen."

"In very good condition."

The beautiful specimen had a look around the pet shop. There were rustling noises everywhere. My Compsognathus looked suddenly very, very hungry. He was breathing faster. He was drooling. And he was looking greedily at the animals in their cages and glass cases, at frogs, lizards, snakes, newts, mice, and birds.

"Funny animals," croaked the Compsognathus.

"You'd like to take them with you, isn't that so?" asked the saleswoman.

"Yes," said the Compsognathus.

"You can buy them," the saleswoman smiled.

"I want those up front," said the Compsognathus. "The green ones."

"We don't need a frog," I said.

"Yes we do," said the Compsognathus. "We need a frog. Right now."

"No."

"Or the little animal over there, the furry one, please."

"The mouse?" asked the saleswoman.

"We don't need a mouse," I said.

"Yes we do," said the Compsognathus. "We absolutely need a mouse. I'm hungry."

The saleswoman opened a bag and gave my dinosaur a small worm.

"Tastes good!" he said.

Then he stared at the mouse again and tried to break loose. Luckily, I'm stronger than he is. But he can squeal horribly when he's not getting his way.

"He already has a collar?" She asked.

"Excuse me?" I held the dinosaur's mouth shut to have some quiet for a moment.

"I asked whether he needed a collar."

"Yes."

"I don't want a collar," squeaked the Compsognathus.

"Dogs wear collars too," said the saleswoman. "It won't bother you at all."

"I don't care what dogs wear. That's their problem. I am a Compsognathus. And a Compsognathus doesn't wear a collar."

"You'll wear it," I said, "or you'll stay at home."

"Gnathus," he hissed furiously.

STRANGE ANIMALS

 I held the door of the pet shop open for the Compsognathus and he ran out of the store with his leash. By now he had forgotten his anger.

I kept him on a very short leash and said, "Be sure to watch out. Cars are dangerous."

"I'm not scared," said the Compsognathus.

"You should be a little scared," I said. "That's sensible."

"All right, I'm a little bit scared. Are you sure the cars stay on the road? Can't they come up here and bite us?"

"Well, they could if they wanted to."

"And how do you know if they want to or not?"

"They're not allowed to."

"You said they could if they wanted to. So what if they want to? Will they come up here then?"

"Sometimes."

"When?"

"You never know."

"Should I run away?"

"That's not necessary."

"Or hide?"

"That's not necessary, either."

"What then?"

"Watch out."

I didn't have to tell the Compsognathus twice. He intended to have a very good look at everything anyway.

I thought we would just be taking an ordinary walk. But that was impossible. A Compsognathus stops to say hello to every car parked on the roadside. He doubted that cars were dangerous.

"Zawinul," he said, "do you think that they can catch anything at all with these rubber claws?"

"Yes. They can."

"Whatever you say."

"I'm not just saying that, I know that."

"If you say so," said the Compsognathus.

Then he waddled alongside of me in silence and looked about, until he said, "Cars are funny animals. They're either standing or running, they can't do much else. I think they look without thinking."

"Cars don't think."

"Maybe they're sleeping with their eyes open."

"Cars don't sleep."

"O? And why don't they look at me?"

"Cars don't look either."

"O? O? O?" said the Compsognathus. "What do they do then, if they don't look?"

I laughed and he didn't like that at all. He just said, "They look. Look for yourself."

"If you like," I said. "They look." But I didn't believe it. And he knew that I didn't believe it.

"Zawinul," he started again, "why is the little blue one looking so cross?"

"Cars always look like that," I said. But that was wrong. They all looked different, some friendly, curious, or pensive, others bored, proud, or insulted. Only the blue car was staring fiercely.

"Maybe it's hungry?" asked the Compsognathus.

"Cars can't be hungry," I said. Maybe this wasn't true anymore since I was called Zawinul and the impossible was not only possible, but happened immediately. I

46

wouldn't have been surprised at all if at that moment the car had hopped forward a couple of feet to the vegetable stall, opened its hood and devoured a pile of lettuce.

"Horrible green stuff!" said the Compsognathus.

Zawinul, I thought, who tells you cars eat lettuce? Maybe cars are carnivores? I didn't want to think about that. Therefore I explained that cars are filled with gas and not interested in food.

"How practical," said the Compsognathus.

Then he stopped, strained at his leash, and wouldn't go another step further.

"I am not a car," he said. " I am hungry."

He wanted to have the bag of mealworms that I had secretly bought for him in the pet shop. Secretly, I thought. But a Compsognathus sees everything.

HOW BIG MUST I GET?

There was no way of picturing my life without the dinosaur anymore. Sometimes I imagined that instead of a Compsognathus, a Torosaurus had crawled out of my Easter egg, and that his head would one day be as big as my room. I tried to imagine how much an animal like that needed to eat. And couldn't it have also been a Kronosaurus, that you have to raise in the bathtub? Or one of those that want to fly? Perhaps a Quetzalcoatlus, who doesn't weigh more than a human being but is a whole lot bigger? A dwarf like the Anurognathus I could have put in a bird cage, but who knows if a dinosaur would put up with that?

49

"What are you thinking?" asked the Compsognathus.

"I'm glad that you're a Compsognathus."

Because even if he went on eating and eating continuously, there would still be an end in sight.

"I'm glad too that I'm a Compsognathus," said the Compsognathus. Then he wrinkled his brow.

"What are you thinking?" I said.

"Why are the flower pots getting smaller?"

I explained to him that the flower pots weren't getting smaller but that he was getting bigger.

"I don't want to get bigger," said the Compsognathus. "I think I'm just right the way I am now."

"You still have to grow a little bit," I said.

"But I don't want to."

When a Compsognathus has got something into his head, there is no use contradicting him. The furrow on his brow hadn't disappeared yet. He asked, "Do you mean it's good to be big?"

Now that I was no longer afraid that he would grow into a huge Diplodocus or something even bigger, I could tell the truth. At least I thought it was the truth. "Of course it's good to be big."

"What is it good for?"

"When you're bigger, you're stronger."

"Why is it good to be stronger?"

I hadn't thought about that yet. "It's better," I said.

"Why better?"

"That's hard to explain."

"Make it short," he said.

"You can defend yourself."

"Defend yourself? Against whom?"

"Against an enemy," I said.

"An enemy? What's that?"

"That's hard to explain," I said again.

"Make it short," he said.

"An enemy is someone who wants to beat you up." I said that because I couldn't think of a better explanation, at least not if it had to be a short one.

51

"Why does the enemy want to beat me up?" asked the Compsognathus.

"Because he's an enemy."

"And why is he an enemy?"

"Because he wants to beat you up. That's logical."

The Compsognathus didn't think that was logical.

So I started from the beginning again. "An enemy is...an enemy is...an enemy is...someone who wants to take something away from you."

"Like what? The leash? Wonderful!" said the Compsognathus.

"Or your food."

He didn't want his food taken away. Not if he was hungry. If he wasn't hungry, he didn't care.

Suddenly I knew what an enemy was, "An enemy is someone who wants to eat you."

"Eat? Me? Honest? That exists? How?"

"Like you ate the fly."

"That wasn't a fly, that was a blowfly."

"Alright," I said. "An enemy wants to eat you just like you ate the blowfly."

"No one can eat me. I'm too big for that."

"An enemy who is bigger and stronger than you can eat you."

"That's terrible!" said the Compsognathus. "The dog next door who is always barking like that, could he eat me?"

"Maybe."

"And how big do I have to get before no one can eat me? As big as you?"

"That's not enough. As big as an elephant, maybe."

"Nobody eats elephants?"

"Hardly."

"How big are elephants?"

"Very big."

"Bigger than cars?"

"Much bigger. And there used to be even bigger animals, once. But even the very biggest were eaten." I showed him a picture of an Apatosaurus.

"The animal looks familiar to me," said the Compsognathus.

Unfortunately, the picture showed the huge Apatosaurus being pulled to the ground by smaller dinosaurs, torn apart and eaten.

"You said," said the Compsognathus, "that if you're big, you can't be eaten."

I hadn't found the answer to his questions yet. Therefore I said, "It's hard to explain . . ."

The Compsognathus didn't want to hear any explanations.

"I'd rather stay the way I am. What's too big is too big. What's too small is too small. And I'm just right."

Have a Taste

 Before dinner the Compsognathus said, "I think I'll become one of the other ones instead."
"What other ones?"
"One of those that eats the others."

"But you are," I said.

"O," said the Compsognathus. "Then I can't be eaten after all."

"I think you can."

"And what can I do about it?"

I thought about that. "Keep your ears and eyes open."

"There's nothing easier than that." The Compsognathus heard and saw everything anyway.

"And what if someone wants to eat me anyway?"

"Then you have to be fast."

"O?" said the Compsognathus, as he dashed out of the kitchen, jumped onto the window sill, threw the cactus on the floor, and asked, "Was that fast enough?" All in one second.

"That's good enough," I said.

"If I want, I can be even faster."

"No doubt," I said, although I doubted it.

"And I could want to be faster than I actually could be," said the Compsognathus. "Now

what about dinner?"

I had bought a big bone with a lot of meat on it for him. He liked to tear off the meat himself. Sometimes he bit into the bone so hard that his teeth broke off.

"Be careful!" I said.

"It doesn't matter. Teeth always grow back again."

Dinosaurs don't have the slightest idea about teeth, I thought. I didn't know yet that he was right.

56

After dinner, the Compsognathus sat on the window sill beneath the potted palm and pulled at the asparagus fern.

"Please don't eat it," I pleaded.

"What do you think of me! I wouldn't touch that green stuff. Do you know what it tastes like? It makes you want to puke!"

Then he frowned and asked, "What do dinosaurs taste like?"

"Omps!" I said.

"Sorry?"

"I said, you'd have to be a paleontologist."

"Stop being silly. Tell me what dinosaurs taste like."

"I haven't tried one yet."

"It's important," he said.

I suggested biting off a piece of his toe.

He suggested we ask the compsologists.

"Who are they?"

"You don't know anything, do you?" the Compsognathus groaned. "Get your books. It'll say in there what I taste like."

It didn't.

The Compsognathus frowned even more, stuck his claws into his mouth, and said, "I think that I taste very good."

"Why shouldn't you?"

"O?" squealed the Compsognathus. "Do you want to eat me?"

I shook my head.

"Honest?"

I nodded.

He thought about it some more and said, "Only what tastes good gets eaten. If you don't want to be eaten, you have to taste bad. Do you understand that?"

I understood.

"And what do I have to do to taste bad?"

"How should I know?"

"Think about it, it's important."

When I think, I usually come up with something. But it's hard to know if the result is correct. "Maybe it would help if you only ate things that taste dreadful," I said.

He looked at me angrily and snarled, "Gnathus!"

Then he jumped up, rushed to the balcony door, and squealed, "O?"

"Meow?" said a voice on the balcony.

"O?"

"A cat," I said.

"But it looks horrible!" said the Compsognathus.

"Cats always look like that."

"It probably tastes like that too."

"That's the cat who's food you eat."

"O? Then it must taste good. Too bad it's too big to eat."

Until this moment the green eyed cat had been staring motionlessly at the Compsognathus. It stopped doing so when a sparrow landed on the railing of the balcony.

"Omps!" whispered the Compsognathus.

The sparrow was sitting there, small and brown, without noticing the cat who was moving only its eyes. When he did, it was too late. The cat leaped and caught the bird.

"Let me go outside," said the Compsognathus.

I shook my head and got his bone out of the refrigerator.

"Bones are boring," said the Compsognathus.

THE STREETCAR

The streetcar stop is at the lower end of Soln-hofener Street. Before I was called Zawinul, that was pretty far away. And now? I count the house numbers imagining that every number means a million years. That's a long time? Not at all. This way it goes a lot faster, and I arrive at the stop in no time.

"I want to come along," said the Compsognathus.

"You can't."

"Why not?" he asked.

"Because you . . . because I . . . because the streetcar . . ."

"Because what?"

Again I could only think of a long row of

dumb excuses. "Don't make such a fuss about it, Zawinul," I said to myself. "He can come along."

"Pretty big," said the Compsognathus when the streetcar came. "Bigger than the other animals, but then again not so fast." While getting on between all the other people's legs he became anxious. Just this once he allowed me to carry him. We sat next to the window. The Compsognathus stretched his neck and stared ahead. There was a woman sitting in front of us. He stretched his neck even more. Every now and then he moved his little black eyes.

"If you bother that woman, we'll get in trouble," I said.

"Shhhhh!" said the Compsognathus.

"What is there to see?"

He turned his head towards my ear and whispered excitedly, "She has a box on her lap."

"What's so exciting about that?"

"The box!" he said. "It's an exciting box. It doesn't have sides."

"Then it is not a box."

"You can see through it," said the Compsognathus. "But still, there's something inside it."

"What is it?"

"Look for yourself," said the Compsognathus.

The woman had a cage on her lap. Inside a little blue bird was hopping about. It hopped from one perch to the other, and then from the other perch to the first one.

"Tastes good," said the Compsognathus.

"Does not taste good," I said.

"I will ask her."

Before I could hold his mouth shut, it had already happened. He tugged at the woman's hat with his sharp teeth. She turned around and looked at me inquiringly.

"You," he said, "can I please ask you something? Why do you have a bird?"

"I beg your pardon," the woman answered, "I do not have a bird."

"But of course you do," said the Compsognathus gently, "or is the animal in your cage not a bird?"

"No, no," she replied. "This is by no means a bird, isn't that so, Kiki? This is a parakeet, isn't that so, Kiki? And now we are going to Mimi's, on vacation, isn't that so, Kiki?"

"Maybe it really isn't a bird," the Compsognathus whispered in my ear, "although he sure looks like one."

Then he tugged at the woman again to say, "I would like to ask something else about the parakeet."

"Please do," the woman said to me. She was smiling now.

"I would like to know, please, whether he tastes as good as the brown ones."

"There aren't any brown parakeets, isn't that so, Kiki? There are only green ones and blue ones."

"Pretty," said the Compsognathus. "And which ones taste better, the green ones or the blue ones?"

The woman had no idea. She took her bird, spoke to him gently, and moved to the front of the street car.

"Do you understand that?" asked the Compsognathus. "What does she need a bird for, if she doesn't even know how he tastes?"

"She doesn't want to eat him. She keeps him for his singing."

"Can he sing?"

"I think so, yes."

"Then he should sing something."

"He doesn't sing in the streetcar."

"Then she doesn't need to take him with her in the streetcar."

"Maybe he can speak."

"In the streetcar?"

"I don't think so."

"I can see you don't have the slightest idea. I'll go up front and ask."

"No you won't," I said. I held him tightly by his shoulders to make him stay seated. We both know that I am stronger than he is. But that doesn't always help. I then try human logic, urgent warnings, or skillful persuasion. Sometimes I try everything together.

The Compsognathus didn't care much for logic if he was being held tightly at the same time. He hated warnings. And he always knew when I was trying to persuade him. I would have had to let go of him first. But if I let go of him, he would have immediately run up front to the woman with the bird. That would mean trouble. And you have to avoid trouble when you're going around with a dinosaur.

"Zawinul," I said to myself, "think carefully about what you are going to do now. You are stronger, you are smarter. So what does that tell you?"

I didn't have time to do any more thinking. The conductor had appeared at the front end of the streetcar. Luckily, I had a ticket. The conductor looked first at the ticket, then at the Compsognathus, then at me.

"Something wrong?" I asked.

He pointed to my dinosaur and said, "Dogs pay half-fare."

"That's not a dog."

"Cats pay half-fare too."

"That's definitely not a cat."

"Whatever it is," he said, "it pays half-fare."

"Where does it say that dinosaurs pay half-fare?"

"It doesn't have to say that anywhere, because dinosaurs no longer exist."

"Ha ha," said the Compsognathus. I discreetly held his mouth shut.

The conductor took a good look at the Compsognathus, and then the matter was clear to him. He said, "Dinosaurs are giant lizards, right? So dinosaurs are tremendously big, right?"

"Or they're tremendously small," said the Compsognathus.

"Giant lizards can't be small. If they're small, they can't be giant, and that's that."

"Zawinul," I said to myself. "Watch out. When a sentence ends with 'that's that,' it's probably wrong. And when a person has said something wrong, he probably won't be willing to discuss the issue. That's the way it usually is.

"Whatever it is," he said, "it pays half-fare."

I tried one more time. "How much do crocodiles pay?"

"That depends on how big they are," he said, but went on, "Nonsense. Crocodiles don't ride streetcars."

"And birds?"

"Birds don't ride streetcars either."

"There's one sitting up front," I said.

"Excuse me?"

"A blue one," I said.

"Tastes good," said the Compsognathus. "Isn't that so, Kiki?"

"Shut up!" I whispered back.

"What was that?" asked the conductor.

"The woman in the second row has a bird," I said. "In the cage. Does he pay?"

"No, not in a cage."

"And if a dinosaur is in a cage, he doesn't have to pay then?"

68

* * *

The conductor had to think about this first, because the case was new to him. I tried to convince him with arguments. I love arguments, even if they don't always lead to conclusions.

"Listen," I said. "A cage takes up much more space than just a bird or a dinosaur. That's logical."

"Logical?" questioned the conductor. "It doesn't matter whether it's logical or not. Animals pay half-fare. And that is an animal, isn't it? When animals are in a cage, they are not animals, but cages, and cages don't pay."

It seemed strange to me that cages could ride for free. The Compsognathus climbed onto my lap, folded himself up, and whispered, "I'm not an animal. I'm a cage."

"That's enough," said the conductor. "We all know that this is an animal. Now let's assume it was a cat. Cats pay when they ride, except when they are riding in a cage. This one here may look like a cage, but he pays. He's as good as a cat."

The Compsognathus didn't like to hear this. When I had paid, he whispered:

"I'm better than a cat."

DINOSAURS DON'T EXIST

 My dinosaur chick had grown up. His legs grew long and longer and his head too. His mouth was pointed and full of teeth that always wanted more to eat. He simply wasn't content with the meat that I bought for him.

"Cans are boring," he said. "And bones are boring too," he added.

He caught flies and dragonflies, and once he even caught a mouse. That was in our basement. And I hadn't even known that mice lived there.

"How did you get into the basement?" I asked.

He laid his head on my hand in a friendly

way and said, "You don't have to know everything, Zawinul."

"Please don't bite!" I said.

Meanwhile he had grown as high as my knee, and luckily I didn't have to worry about him getting much bigger. He was enough for me as he was. My life would have been easier if a chicken or a parrot had hatched out of that Easter egg.

"Zawinul," I'd say to myself every day, "why can't you have a bird like other people? Why, of all things, does it have to be a dinosaur?"

"A Compsognathus," said the Compsognathus.

"I know," I said.

Because once you have him, you don't just have him for ten minutes or two hours. You have him all the time. Early in the morning he would get up and fetch his collar and leash from the hook. That's something a chicken wouldn't do. A chicken does not want to go for walks. A dinosaur does.

"A Compsognathus," said the Compsognathus.

"I know," I said.

72

I have tried to leave him at home. It doesn't work. As soon as I'm back, as soon as I've calmed him, the neighbors ring at the door, look at me angrily, and ask why my dog yowls for hours.

"I don't have a dog," I tell them.

"What are those strange noises?"

"It must be the water-pipe," I say. "Or the radio. I forgot to turn it off." But soon I won't be able to think of any more excuses. So I've gotten into the habit of taking him along when I have to go out of the house.

The Compsognathus was already tugging hard on his leash when the phone rang. My friend was calling to inquire about my life with a dinosaur.

"Pretty ompsy," I said.

"And what does that mean?" asked my friend.

"I'll explain it to you some other day. I don't have time right now."

"What was that?" asked my friend, because the Compsognathus was so loud.

"I'll call you back!" I yelled into the receiver.

73

The Compsognathus sat on the telephone and asked, "Why are you yelling like that, Zawinul?"

I tucked him under my jacket until we were out in the street. Outside people usually mistook him for a kangaroo. When we walked down Solnhofen Street in single file, he at the front end and I at the back end of the leash, people would stop. Even men who were in a hurry took the time to stare at him. Again there was one who inquired whether the Compsognathus was a kangaroo, even though today most people have seen what a kangaroo looks like and should know they are completely different.

"Not at all," insisted the next one. "Kangaroos have pouches, and I don't see a pouch."

"Or an armadillo?"

"Armadillos have armor," said another.

"Nonsense. That's just the name. Armadillos don't have armor."

"But a rattlesnake has a rattle and a striped bass has stripes."

Then they thought about whether a reindeer has reins and a horn toad a horn.

"Otherwise they wouldn't have those names," one voice said.

74

"If that's true, then a butterfly flies butter," another one said.

They discussed whether the blindworm is blind or a hermitcrab really a hermit. But they agreed about the duck-billed platypus. It has a bill. They were no longer paying attention to us and we took the opportunity to slink away. From a distance we could still hear their loud voices.

"Maybe it's an ostrich after all?" one of them said, having once seen an emu long ago. We heard the others laughing at him. Then we arrived at the park.

We both liked the park. But the Compsognathus didn't like walking on a leash. Walking isn't the right word, either. He waddled alongside me with his long legs. But that wasn't what he wanted. He wanted to run.

"Gnathus!" he said.

"What is that supposed to mean?"

"It's supposed to mean, Zawinul, would you be kind enough to remove this stupid dog-leash right away."

"I know that you are not a dog," I said.

"Then get on with it."

"It's forbidden," I said.

"What does forbidden mean?"

"That you're not allowed to do it."

"Why not?"

"Because people or other animals will get frightened if you run around here."

"Frightened? Who?"

"Birds, mice, butterflies. They think you want to eat them."

"But that's what they're there for!" said the Compsognathus.

I showed him a sign standing by the path. It showed a dog obediently walking on his leash.

"I am not a dog," said the Compsognathus.

"Woof! Woof! Woof!" I heard behind me. The voice belonged to a dog. He wasn't walking obediently on a leash like the dog on the sign. He didn't even have a leash. He was not partic-

76

ularly big, and not particularly small, but particularly furious.

I know that dogs are reasonable creatures,
but nevertheless I'm always a little frightened of
them, especially when they bare their teeth and
snarl. My dinosaur seized the opportunity to
break loose and attack the dog. The dog hadn't
counted on that. He ran off, and the Compsognathus ran after him. I ran too, trying to catch
him. I ran down the paths, I flung myself under
every bush where I thought I heard a squeal or
a growl or a shriek. But I found no animal that
had such beautiful legs, such a long tail, and

such sharp claws. After an hour I gave up and went home alone.

At home it was strangely quiet. There was no one there who needed to be fed, no one who sharpened his claws on the sofa, and no one who clung to the curtains with his claws and swung back and forth in front of the window.

That evening I went to bed and couldn't fall asleep. I was sad and wished that the Compsognathus with his lizard skin and his difficult questions was lying in his basket under the bed. I had become used to the fact that every time I was almost asleep, he woke me up again by saying, "Psst! I have to ask you something!"

"Please ask me tomorrow," I would tell him. "Now I want to sleep."

And he would say, "Tomorrow I'll have forgotten it."

But tonight he wasn't lying under my bed keeping me from falling asleep, and that kept me from falling asleep. Besides, I was thinking of him alone in the park now, in the

dark night. Nowadays the nights aren't as warm as they used to be when dinosaurs were living. Maybe he was sitting somewhere in the ground ivy, shivering.

Or perhaps he was running around, and the other animals in the park were shivering because the Compsognathus was hungry. I have seldom slept as badly.

"Zawinul," I said to myself, "this is exactly what you wished for: a life without dinosaurs." I really had wished for it. More than once. But for an animal who had been born on my window sill to wander about in the night all by himself, that I really didn't want.

The next day I went to the park again. I was determined to find him, even if I had to crawl around under the bushes all day and all night.

That wasn't necessary because the Compsognathus was sitting in exactly the same spot where he had run off to bite the dog. He had his leash in his mouth, held it out to me, and said reproachfully, "Where have you been all this time, Zawinul?"

"Me?" I said.

The Compsognathus strolled along before me on his leash as if he had never done anything else. People stopped again, like they always do when they see a dinosaur.

"Look at that animal there," they said.

"I am not an 'animalthere,'" squeaked the Compsognathus. "I am a Compsognathus."

"A compsowhat?"

"No compsowhat."

"Then what?"

"A compso-gnathus."

"Oh. And what is that, a gnathus?"

"A dinosaur."

When I said that, they usually turned around quickly and walked on. We could still hear them muttering, "Dinosaurs don't exist."

"What is that supposed to mean?" asked the Compsognathus.

"It's supposed to mean that dinosaurs are extinct."

"And what is that supposed to mean?"

"That the Compsognathus existed one hundred and forty million years ago and that he doesn't anymore."

"Are you sure?" asked the Compsognathus. "It could always be that someplace, where no one has looked, one remains."

"I don't think so."

"And why not?"

"You wouldn't understand."

"Zawinul," said the Compsognathus, "are you trying to say that you don't know?"

That was exactly what I was trying to say. But it isn't my fault that I don't know. Nobody knows. Some people believe the dinosaurs were too big anyway and simply couldn't survive very long. But, in fact, the opposite is true. The dinosaurs did last an especially long time. Some researchers imagine that volcanic eruptions devastated the

earth and darkened the sky. Others believe a meteorite fell onto the earth. And still others say they have found the craters of two meteorites which fell onto the earth at more or less the same time.

All this is possible. But the extinction of the dinosaurs is a much longer story. The Compsognathus wanted to hear it. But to be honest, I didn't know all the details.

I said, "For a long time there were always new dinosaurs. Others died out. Gradually, after a while, there weren't any anymore. Do you understand that?"

"Of course," said the Compsognathus. "Dying out is the simplest thing on earth."

"On the contrary. It's a very complicated thing."

"How do you know?" he said. "Were you there by any chance?"

"Not at the time."

"I thought so."

"But I'm here today."

"You said there aren't any dinosaurs left to die out."

"There are other animals."

"Who die out?" He didn't believe me.

"Many animals become extinct."

"Will Baxter become extinct too?"

"I don't think so."

"Too bad. But I should have expected it. An animal that barks like that can't die out."

"You don't know anything about it."

I shouldn't have said that.

The Compsognathus screeched as loudly as he could, "Am I extinct or are you?"

Going to the Museum

People often say it's a great thing to have an animal around the house. I say it can also be a nuisance, especially when that animal is a Compsognathus. Although it's common knowledge that even a dinosaur should be washed every now and then, he wouldn't allow it. All I had to do was turn the faucet on and he would start squealing and run away. I'd run after him until I caught him.

"Wait a second with the water," said the Compsognathus.

"Why?"

"I have to think first."

"Are you crazy?"

"Do you have to be crazy to think?" said the Compsognathus.

It wasn't easy washing him. He could move so fast that I hardly knew how to hold on to him. When his skin was all wet and slippery from the water and the soap, he usually managed to jump away and hide someplace where no drop of water could ever reach him.

He only showed up again after I had washed too, and turned off the water. And then, when I wanted to read the newspaper, he would first jump on my lap, then on my newspaper, and squeak, "Reading is boring!"

"Maybe for you," I said.

"I have to ask you something," he said next.

"Please ask me something simple!"

"How many dinosaurs are there?"

"There aren't any dinosaurs at all anymore."

"That's not what I mean," said my dinosaur. "I want to know how many there used to be."

"No one knows exactly. Hundreds. And every year there are more."

"You said there aren't any dinosaurs anymore. How can there always be more?"

I explained to him how the paleontologists are out in great numbers, searching for the remains of dinosaurs.

"And? Do they find any?"

"Many."

"And what do they do with them?"

"They put them back together and try to find out something about the lives of the dinosaurs."

"Very interesting," said the Compsognathus.

He wanted to see the dinosaurs that the researchers had dug up and put together again.

"You're lucky," I said, "there's an exhibition at the museum. We can go there tomorrow."

"Tomorrow."

The Compsognathus squealed so loudly that I was afraid the neighbors would ring again and ask what I was doing to my dog. I put my jacket on and took the leash. He stopped squealing right away.

When we reached the museum ticket counter the Compsognathus and I were the only visitors there at that moment.

"Two," I said.

I was only given one ticket.

"Two, please," I said.

The woman at the desk leaned forward. She pushed her glasses down a little and looked at me. She looked all around me. Then she said, "I don't see anyone else."

"There is no one else," I said.

The Compsognathus pinched my leg.

"Don't make such a fuss," I hissed. The woman had heard me. I could tell from her face.

"I'd like two tickets anyway, please," I said. "If that's possible?"

"Lots of things are possible," she said, shaking her head.

We weren't inside yet, though. I held the Compsognathus on a short leash, led him to the entrance as discreetly as possible, and held out the tickets to the man standing there. He pointed to a sign. It showed a dog and two lines crossing the dog out. I pretended I hadn't seen his gesture and pulled the Compsognathus a few steps further. The man stretched out his arm and said, "Dogs aren't allowed."

"Omps!" I said.

"What was that?" said the man.

"I said, that's not a dog."

"Really? I thought you said something totally different. But horses, cats, and hamsters aren't allowed either."

88

"That's not a hamster."

"I can see that for myself," he said. "I know what a hamster looks like."

"Presumably, zebra finches and kangaroos aren't allowed either."

"Quite right." The man stared at the Compsognathus. "Hold on a second," he said then. "Is that supposed to be a kangaroo by any chance?"

"No."

"Too bad." He added, "I would have liked to pet a kangaroo. Just once in my life. I would let a kangaroo in, even though it's forbidden. But if it's not a kangaroo, what is it then?"

"A Compsognathus," said the Compsognathus.

And I added, "Here's his entrance ticket." I regretted that we hadn't said he was a kangaroo.

The man pretended he hadn't heard the voice. "What is it?" he repeated, looking at me the way people do who guard entrances and don't want to let others in, even though they have a valid entrance ticket.

"A dinosaur," I said.

"Dinosaurs don't exist," said the man.

"Go ahead and let him in. He's extinct."

"Extinct animals are forbidden too," said the man. Then he stared at the Compsognathus. "Extinct? I see, I see. And if he's so extinct, then what's he still doing here?"

"He wants to look at the dinosaurs."

"That's what they all want," said the man.

"Longlegs," I said, "we're leaving."

For once, the Compsognathus agreed with me entirely. When we were outside he started thinking again. He stopped and frowned until he finally said, "This person knows nothing about dinosaurs."

"That's right," I said. "And you found out."

"How do we get into the exhibition now?"

"Very simple." I hid the Compsognathus under my jacket, stroked his long neck, and said, "Don't omps!"

He curled his tail around my back and was very still. Then I went back inside with my slightly bulging jacket, and when we were in the large auditorium I opened the zipper. He stuck his head out and with his black eyes he looked without ompsing once.

We were surrounded by many prehistoric animals. Some were tremendously big. And even the medium-sized animals were still huge.

Full of doubts, the Compsognathus looked first at the skeletons, then at me, and whispered, "Are those really dinosaurs? I mean, do you think they look like me?"

He stretched his beautiful leg, equipped with claws, skin, muscles, tendons, veins, and everything else that's necessary, out of my jacket so that I could compare it to the legs in the exhibition, and looked me straight in the face.

"Yes," I said.

He just wrinkled his brow and growled, "Gnathus."

"You're right," I said. "You're much more beautiful."

That made him feel better.

After a short while he looked at me again. He made a question-mark with his neck and whispered, "Maybe I'm not a dinosaur after all."

"Yes you are."

"You're just saying that to make me feel better."

"What are you then, if you're not a dinosaur, huh?"

"How should I know? Would you know what you were if you weren't a human being?"

I hadn't thought about that yet.

"Then do it now, Zawinul!" said the Compsognathus.

I thought about it and said, "I don't know."

"That's just what I thought."

He looked around and marveled. "Quite a lot of bones!"

I nodded.

"Two thousand," said the Compsognathus thoughtfully, "and more."

They were all from China.

"Is China far away?"

"Very far. I'll show you at home on the globe."

92

I wondered how all those bones had gotten from China to the museum.

"In sixty-one crates," said the Compsognathus.

"How do you know that?"

"Very simple. It says so in the newspaper."

A dinosaur that reads the newspaper? Zawinul, I thought, something's wrong here.

"Let go of me," the Compsognathus suddenly shrieked. Immediately, I clapped my hand over his beautiful loud mouth. It was too late. The attendant appeared in the doorway and looked at me as if I had eaten one of the precious bones. I closed my jacket and strolled slowly on, holding his mouth shut discreetly with an elbow, trying to look like other people who don't have a Compsognathus wrapped around their belly. It took a while before the attendant would let me out of his sight.

"Don't ever do that again!" I whispered.

"There they are!" he whispered. We were standing before a glass case. Inside it, a prehistoric landscape spread itself out in an unreal light. The whole wide land was full of dinosaurs in different sizes, peacefully grazing and picking the foliage from the trees. From a forest with strange trees a family of tyrannosaurs burst out as if, at any moment, they would pounce on anyone who wasn't fast enough.

"Beautiful!" said the Compsognathus.

"Is this what it looked like when the earth was full of dinosaurs?" I asked him. Secretly, I hoped that he could still remember something.

"I don't think so," said the Compsognathus.

For a long time he continued to look into the case. Then he creased his brow and whispered, "You said the other dinosaurs were much bigger than me. And these are much smaller."

"They're just models."

"That's what I thought," said the Compsognathus. He preferred to look at the real ones, even if they consisted only of bones.

A lot of dinosaurs were assembled in the exhibition. We stopped under the largest. He was longer than a streetcar. He stood on four legs, and when you looked up at his head, the tip of his tail was pretty far away.

"This really exists?" whispered the Compsognathus.

"It existed."

"Is it practical?" he whispered. "How can

94

the tail hear what the head is thinking when it's so far away?"

"I have no idea," I said. "Maybe the tail could think on its own."

"What's it called?"

"The head or the tail?"

"Stop being silly," said the Compsognathus looking at the plaque put up to explain the tremendous bones. "Read to me instead."

"Mamenchisaurus," I read, "born one hundred and sixty million years ago; length sixty-six feet, height twelve feet, weight thirty tons."

"And you believe that, Zawinul?"

"Of course."

"Fifteen tons at most," said the Compsognathus.

"Now don't you tell me you can remember the Mamenchisaurus."

The Compsognathus was annoyed. All he said was, "Don't you read the newspaper?"

"I will read the newspaper tomorrow," I said, "if you stop bothering me when I do so."

"Okay," he said. "There's just one more thing I'd like to know: What is a ton?"

"That's hard to explain."

"Then don't. Let's just say ten times as heavy as I am."

"No, much heavier. Maybe three hundred times."

"Nobody can figure that out," said the Compsognathus.

THERE IS ALWAYS AN EGG

"Zawinul," said the Compsognathus when we were home. "Where did you dig me up?"

"I didn't dig you up."

"Then where did I come from, if you didn't dig me up?"

"Out of an egg," I said truthfully. But, as often happens with the truth, it sounded unlikely.

"Out of what kind of an egg?" asked the Compsognathus, and I could tell that he didn't believe me.

"Out of an Easter egg that was lying on my window sill."

"Okay," he said. "And how did my egg get on your window sill?"

"I found it in the garden, under the daffodils."

"And how did it end up under the daffodils?"

"No idea."

"It's important."

"Maybe the egg was lying in the ground all the time and worked its way up now."

"A hundred and forty million years?" asked the Compsognathus.

"Why not?"

"Zawinul," said the Compsognathus. "You can't believe that."

I didn't know if I should believe it.

The Compsognathus would not stop thinking about it. He said, "Are you sure that I hatched out of an egg?"

"Yes. Why?"

"Maybe I also came in a crate from China. Like the other dinosaurs."

"No," I said. "No one has found dinosaurs like you in China yet."

"And where did they find dinosaurs like me?"

"In Solnhofen," I said.

"And that's not in China?"

"Definitely not. It's in Germany."

The Compsognathus said, "If only I knew whether I could believe you."

99

"Solnhofen...," he mumbled. "China...? Doesn't that sound much better? Or Paris? What can you expect to find in Solnhofen."

"You," I said, "and the beautiful Archaeopteryx."

"What's that?" asked the Compsognathus.

"A kind of small pigeon," I said, "with wings and feathers."

"Tastes good," said the Compsognathus.

"Too late."

"Extinct?"

"Extinct."

"Zawinul," said the Compsognathus, "If only I knew whether I could believe you."

Then he wanted to see the egg which he hatched from. Luckily, I had kept it. With that, I thought, all doubts would be removed. I was mistaken.

"Who broke it?" he asked.

"No one can get out of an egg without breaking it."

He looked at the eggshell, let some furrows appear on his brow, and then started to laugh heartily.

"Zawinul," he said with a little concern, "you can't be right in your head. This is not my egg." He lifted a foot and tried to step into the egg. "Do you see this?"

"Yes."

"Can you explain to me how an entire Compsognathus is supposed to have been inside this puny little egg, if my foot doesn't even fit in now?"

"I can explain that to you very easily."

"O? O? O?" said the Compsognathus.

But I didn't even try to explain it to him.

Next he said, "Maybe you're just imagining about the eggs, and I came from China in a crate after all."

"Why should someone send me a crate from China, can you tell me that?"

"No. But can you tell me why someone shouldn't do it?"

I couldn't.

"If you don't believe that," continued the Compsognathus thinking it over, "then perhaps it was the other way around."

"Which other way around?"

"I didn't come to you, but you to me, Zawinul. In a crate from China."

"Nonsense," I said.

"You don't believe in crates, then," said the Compsognathus.

I explained to him that I was perfectly sure that I did not come from a crate, whether it was from China or anywhere else.

"Very well," he said, "I'll believe you, if you show me your egg."

"My egg?"

"Now don't pretend to be dumber than you are, Zawinul. The egg you hatched out of must have been pretty big."

He was certain that human beings laid

102

eggs. "You're trying to make fun of me," he said. "The little human beings have to hatch out of something, don't they? Out of little cars, maybe? Like the big human beings, who always come out of big cars?"

"Not out of cars," I said. "Out of their mother."

"Without a shell?"

"Yes."

"Don't they break?"

I hadn't thought about that.

Who knows, maybe it would be more practical if little brothers and sisters came with an eggshell. Then they wouldn't make so much noise. And they would make much less trouble too, if they were properly packed up until they were big. But then a mother would have to sit around on her egg the whole time.

"That's not necessary," said the Compsognathus.

"Chickens do it though."

"But chickens are crazy," said the Compsognathus. "One simply lays eggs in the sun, and the chicks come out on their own."

"But that's not what chickens do."

"Why don't you try it out sometime."

"I don't think that would work," I said.

"Why shouldn't it work?"

"Because humans can't lay eggs."

"It can't be so hard," said the Compsognathus. "Any titmouse can lay eggs."

"Titmice can. Humans can't."

The Compsognathus wrinkled his brow and seriously wondered why human beings hadn't died out long ago, if they couldn't even lay eggs.

"I don't think you will exist for long, if you are so impractical," he said.

"But we've been here for quite a while now."

"How long?"

"At least a few million years."

"You think that's a long time?"

"Well...," I said.

He looked at the two eggs that were still lying in the nest. "Blue rabbits and goldfish," he said. "When will they hatch?"

I explained to him that these were Easter eggs, that Easter eggs are boiled, and that nothing hatches out of boiled eggs.

"If I hatched," he said," they'll hatch too."

"But blue rabbits don't exist."

"Extinct?" asked the Compsognathus.

"No, never existed."

"How do you know?"

Yes, how did I know? I didn't know. But I knew that I knew.

"And golden fish don't exist either?"

"Yes, they do."

"But not out of eggs???"

"Not out of such big eggs."

"Maybe it's going to be a very big gold-fish," said the Compsognathus.

"No."

"If golden fish exist," he said, "then blue rabbits exist too. Everything else is illogical."

DOES THAT EXIST?

 "It's a pity that there are no blue rabbits," sighed the Compsognathus.

"Yes."

"And there are no dinosaurs, either," he continued to sigh. "Stegosaurs, Protoceratops, apatosaurs don't exist..."

"Yes," I said. "It's a pity that there are animals that don't exist anymore."

"And there are no goldfish, either." He just kept on sighing.

"Yes, there are," I said. "Goldfish exist."

"Where?" The Compsognathus jumped up.

"There isn't one here right now."

"What a pity!"

"But goldfish do exist. Even if there isn't one here."

"I'm glad they do!" said the Compsognathus. "There's just one thing I don't understand, Zawinul. Are there only those animals that exist, or are there also animals that don't exist?"

"Naturally, there are only those that exist. That's logical. And those that aren't there, don't exist. That's logical, too."

"That means there are only those that exist?"

"Of course."

"And those that aren't there don't exist?"

"Exactly. How can there be something that doesn't exist?"

"There can," said the Compsognathus.

"There can't," I said.

"Before, you said yourself that there are dinosaurs that don't exist."

"Omps," I said.

"Don't 'omps,' Zawinul," said the Compsognathus. "Think."

"I said that there are dinosaurs that don't exist anymore."

"So they don't exist," said the Compsognathus.

"Exactly."

108

"Therefore, things that don't exist, exist after all!"

"No. There are simply things that don't exist."

"Isn't that the same?"

"Not at all."

"Is that logical?" asked the Compsognathus.

What should I say to that? Just one word, and that was:

Everything's Topsy-Turvy

Since this dinosaur arrived, time passed faster than ever before. Summer had hardly begun when it was over already. The leaves were falling from the trees. The Compsognathus believed they did this to please him. He jumped, hopped, and skipped. Or he stood very still and listened. And as soon as something rustled anywhere, he jumped off to grab it. If it turned out to be alive, he ate it up. If not, he dropped it. He was so steady on his two legs he could jump without thinking much about it. He didn't even need to turn around. If something rustled behind him, he turned while jumping.

Then winter came. The Compsognathus stood in the doorway, stuck out his nose, and said, "What's this supposed to be?"

"It's winter," I said.

"Must this be? I'm cold!"

"A dinosaur can't be cold," I said.

"That may be true. But I am a Compsognathus, and a Compsognathus is cold. Do you want to feel?"

"You're all warm."

"Of course I'm warm. That's why I'm cold."

Outside it was snowing.

"Pretty," said the Compsognathus. "But too cold."

He didn't mind if we stayed at home. It also didn't bother him if he bothered me.

Whatever I did, the Compsognathus was there. When I tidied my things, he watched. And he was faster than I was. If I wanted to

112

get my shoes out from under the bed, he reached them before I did and ran with them into the kitchen. He could spread piles of paper out on the floor as fast as lightning. When I wanted to carry a plate into the kitchen, he already had it in his claws and was trying to bite off the rim. I don't clean up often. But every now and then it's necessary.

"Is that work?" he asked.

"Yes."

"Work is nice," said the Compsognathus. "I could watch for hours."

"You call that watching?" I told him, "I think you're in the way."

For once, he jumped up on the bed and just watched until I was done. I was satisfied. On the bed, except for the dinosaur, there were only bedclothes, on the table only paper, and on the floor nothing at all. It looked wonderful.

"I like this a lot better already," I said.

"I want to work too," said the Compsognathus.

He started to pull all sorts of things out from under the bed. Lots of wood appeared, which belonged to a chair. I should have glued it together again a long time ago. It had been lying under the bed since the first chapter.

"Omps!" said the Compsognathus.

"Stop it right now!" I said.

But he didn't stop. I tried to prevent him, but again, he was faster than I was. And he found much more under the bed than wood: a comb, a ball-point pen, and clothes. I don't want to list everything. Finally he pulled out my suitcase and took out every single object I needed for travelling. When he was finished, the room looked worse than when we started: A complete mess.

The Compsognathus looked at the result of his work and said, "I like this a lot better already."

I liked it less.

"Utter chaos!" I yelled.

"What do you mean?" asked the Compsognathus.

"Everything's topsy-turvy!" I groaned.

He looked at me sympathetically and groaned, "Topsy-turnips! Horrible green stuff!"

"How am I supposed to tidy this up again?"

"I don't know anything about turnips," said the Compsognathus as he jumped on the bed. He remained seated there and watched me. It was hard work trying to sort out the papers. When I tried to shove the wood under the bed, I got a splinter in my thumb. It bled.

"Tastes good!" said the Compsognathus.

I grumbled, "Gnathus!" then put a band-aid on my thumb, and continued to work.

"Zawinul," said my dinosaur pensively after half an hour, "you shouldn't work so much."

I still wasn't finished yet and muttered angrily, "Cut it out! You don't even exist! You're extinct!"

"Whatever you say," said the Compsognathus.

Shut Your Beak

The trouble just didn't stop. The neighbors rang to say they had just about enough of my dog. The fact that I didn't have a dog didn't interest them. They wanted to know who had bitten their dog Baxter when he was on the porch.

"It wasn't me," I said.

My dinosaur had learned a lot. He could pull shoe-laces out of shoes. He could hide in jacket sleeves or pant legs. He could find a new hiding place for the house-key every day. My dinosaur had learned to open the refrigerator. And when a dinosaur opens a refrigerator, he empties it out. He had also learned to open the door to the balcony and one day when I heard shrill shrieks on the balcony I found him fighting the cat who decided to come visit us again. I poured a bucket of water over the two animals and dragged the furious Compsognathus into the room.

"That stupid cat scratched me!" he said.

"And you didn't scratch?"

"Biting is better!" said the Compsognathus.

The doorbell rang. Some people that I don't know told me to keep a better eye on my dog. Their cat had come home with its fur all bloody. I didn't have the courage to tell them I didn't own a dog.

I needed to talk to a human being. I called my friend Zawinul who had been so kind as to let me have his name, and is therefore no longer called Zawinul.

"What should I do?" I asked. "I have a dinosaur who messes everything up. You know how dinosaurs are. He won't even let me read the newspaper."

"Wait until he falls asleep," answered my friend. "Then you can read in peace."

"Is that all you can come up with?"

"Yes," he said.

If he were still called Zawinul, he would have come up with something better. "I can come up with an idea like that by myself. I don't need to call you up for that."

"If that's the way it is," he said, "then don't."

"You can count on that."

Nobody has any idea how a dinosaur sleeps. Mine never really slept at all. Not the way we sleep. He was constantly ready to wake up as soon as anything exciting happened. To his mind everything I did was exciting, therefore I couldn't even read the newspaper without him bugging me.

"Why don't you turn the page?" he would ask all of a sudden, when I thought he was fast asleep. He had been lying there very still, only twitching his claws now and then. I imagined how he was dreaming of the giant dragon-flies of the Mesozoic era or of tiny furry animals who scurried about in the rubble and were hard to catch. He smacked his lips in his sleep and at the same time he said, "Reading is boring."

"Shut that beak of yours!" I wanted to go on reading.

"What's a beak?"

"It's what a bird has in the middle of its face."

"I'm not a bird," said the Compsognathus.

"Almost," I said.

"But not quite."

"Keep it shut anyway. Please."

"Beak's a funny word," said the Compsognathus. "Beeeak! Beeeak! Beak-beak-beak!"

120

"Quiet!"

"Omps!" said the Compsognathus.

"Please don't say 'Omps,' either."

"Why did you say 'shut that beak' if I don't even have a beak?"

"I just felt like it."

"In my case you'll have to say something else."

"With pleasure. Shut your gob."

"I don't have a gob," said the Compsognathus.

"Then shut your trap."

"I don't have a trap either."

"Then shut your mouth."

"Why?"

"I want to read."

"You could have said so sooner. Go ahead and read. It doesn't bother me," said the Compsognathus.

It's all right for a dinosaur to talk. I decided to stop reading and repair the chair first. I got the pincers, the hammer, and the nails. I also got the glue and the screw-clamps. This is something a dinosaur will enjoy. First of all he will spill all the nails. Then he will hit his claws with the hammer. Finally, his teeth will get all sticky with the glue. But that doesn't

121

bother a Compsognathus. If he breaks a tooth, it grows back.

A short while later, the chair in front of me was looking very much like it did before. Immediately, the Compsognathus jumped up on it, stretched out on the seat, and the chair broke down again because the glue wasn't dry yet. I started over and when I was done, I tied the Compsognathus to the bed with his dog-leash.

"I'm not a dog," he grumbled.

"I know."

"Shut your beak!" said the Compsognathus.

"I don't have a beak."

He was furious. He tore at the leash and barked, "I'm not a dog!"

"Stop it," I said. "I've had enough. Dinosaurs don't exist."

* * *

122

Ever since I started walking around with a Compsognathus I've had nothing but trouble. People stopped in the street. The neighbors thought I was crazy. My friends groaned when I called. "That's all nonsense!" They would say.

The Compsognathus wouldn't let me think about anything else but the Compsognathus. And when he was sleeping, I thought about not being able to think about anything else. It was impossible to do sensible things anymore.

"Dinosaurs don't exist," I repeated.

"Except for me," said the Compsognathus.

"And whether you really exist—I'm not so sure. I think I just made you up."

"You could do that? Make me up?"

"I can make up a lot more."

The Compsognathus became alarmed. "Maybe you made me up all wrong."

That is possible. One hundred and forty million years is a long time. And I don't make up a dinosaur every day. It's quite possible I made a mistake.

"Listen Longlegs," I said. "I tried hard to make you the right way. But it's not easy. The Compsognathus lived a long time ago, when there weren't any human beings yet."

"And now there are human beings?"

"You can see that for yourself," I said.

"Maybe you just made them up too," said the Compsognathus. "If you can make up dinosaurs, you can also make up human beings."

"I don't believe that I made human beings up. But to be honest, I don't know what to believe anymore."

"Maybe," the Compsognathus continued, "if you made up human beings, you also made up the cars and the streetcar? Could you do that?"

"I don't know."

"And the streets they drive on. And the trees on the roadside. And the birds in the trees, and the songs that the birds sing. Could you do that?"

"I don't know."

"Maybe all this doesn't exist. The chair doesn't exist. And the newspaper that you want to read doesn't exist either."

"Could I do that?"

"Why not?" questioned the Compsognathus.

124

"Because it's difficult."

"It can't be that difficult to make it up."

He was right, I thought. It only gets difficult when it really has to be there. You can make up a lot of things, especially when your name is Zawinul.

125

Then the Compsognathus grinned and said, "And you don't exist either, because you only made yourself up."

"Shut your beak!" I said. At the same time, I thought: Who knows if he isn't right after all?

126

See what this has led to. I don't know whether I made myself up, or whether I just imagined that I made myself up.

I went to the window and looked outside. It's a good place for thinking. I looked up at the sky for a while, where the clouds wander, and thought I'd eventually come up with something. After a few minutes I did. Zawinul, I said to myself, don't worry. You exist. Because if you didn't exist, you couldn't be standing here, watching the clouds, and wondering whether you exist or not.

THERE ARE NO BLUE RABBITS

 It was noon time. The house was quiet except for the familiar rustling, door-slamming, ringing, barking and music from all directions. Once again I stood at the window and thought: This can't be. I looked at the window sill once more. When I looked at it for the third time, it was the same.

"Zawinul," I said, "in front of you is the green Easter nest with two ancient Easter eggs. One has a goldfish painted on it and the other blue rabbits. Everything else is impossible."

Nevertheless, the eggs were gone. There were only shells left, empty ones.

"Omps!" I said.

I had a hunch. But I didn't want to think about it.

The Compsognathus was squatting in front of the sofa. He had something red in his hand. This he put in his mouth and swallowed. He smacked his lips. Then he glanced in my direction and whispered, "Goldfish aren't golden after all. They're red."

"Do you mean to tell me that you just ate a goldfish?"

"Tastes good," whispered the Compsognathus.

"Omps," I said.

"Don't 'omps.' Shut your beak," whispered the Compsognathus.

"I don't have a beak," I said.

"Shut it anyway," whispered the Compsognathus.

"Hey, what's going on?"

"Shhhhhh!"

Something's wrong here, I thought. A Compsognathus who whispers all the time is impossible. He hadn't budged once and was staring under the sofa where it was very dark. Finally I could hear what was going on. Something under the sofa was scratching. And when something is scratching under the sofa, there must be someone doing the scratching.

130

That's logical. I lay down flat on my stomach. At first I saw nothing. Then I saw a blue ear. Then nothing again.

"Zawinul," I said, "this can't be."

The Compsognathus was sitting there, motionless and staring. I sat next to him just as motionless and stared too.

Have you gone crazy? I asked myself. I wanted to see the blue rabbit that was sitting under the sofa. If indeed he was sitting there. Unfortunately, it was too dark to recognize anything so I got a flashlight. I don't have to describe what I saw next. Everyone knows what a little rabbit looks like. And everyone knows what blue looks like. He didn't seem scared at all. He looked at us cheerfully and wrinkled his nose continuously at breath-taking speed.

"Why does he do that?" asked the Compsognathus.

"Rabbits always do that," I said.

"It's driving me mad," said the Compsognathus.

The rabbit was still small and didn't know much. But luckily he seemed to understand that the best thing he could do was to stay under the sofa. The Compsognathus didn't take his eyes off him. I pushed the green straw from the Easter nest into his den, so that he could make himself comfortable.

"Thank you very much," he said. He was a somewhat awkward blue rabbit, and it took him a long time to build himself a nest.

The Compsognathus turned to me and whispered, "You see, Zawinul? There are blue rabbits after all. Who was right then, you or me?"

What was I supposed to say to that?

"Besides, you claimed that rabbits don't hatch out of eggs."

132

"Because they don't."

The Compsognathus looked at me and smiled, as if I had said something very dumb.

"May I ask you for something to eat, Mr. Zawinul?" asked the rabbit.

How could I forget. Even blue rabbits get hungry. Luckily, they are not carnivores, and they are happy if you give them carrots and dandelions.

"Horrible green stuff," said the Compsognathus.

"Thank you very much," said the rabbit.

"Zawinul," said the Compsognathus, "why does the rabbit talk so funny?"

"Rabbits always do that," I said.

He said nothing. But when I asked him whether he liked the blue rabbit, he nodded pensively and whispered, "I love rabbits."

"Maybe you can become friends."

"Maybe," said the Compsognathus. "But not if he's always wrinkling his nose."

Wrinkles appeared on his brow, first one, then two, then three. He was thinking, intensely so. When a dinosaur is thinking, he should be left alone. He hadn't completely finished thinking when he murmured, "The question is, what do blue rabbits taste like?"

133

This was one of those questions that can't be answered by just thinking them over.

"Probably they taste blue."

"You can't taste colors," I said.

"Is that supposed to mean blue rabbits taste exactly like green rabbits?"

"I presume so."

"So you don't know."

"Of course not."

"And can you tell me what the colors are for, if you can't taste them?"

This was another one of those things I didn't know.

The Compsognathus wanted to know. He began fishing under the sofa with his front legs. Luckily for the rabbit, his front legs were too short.

"Help me get him out."

"No," I said. "Maybe he'll come out by himself if you say something nice to him."

However, I hoped the rabbit would stay under the sofa. I wanted to keep him, too. Pets, people say, have a soothing effect. They say this especially of fish. But now that our fish had been eaten before I even had seen him, I assumed that the rabbit wouldn't make any noise either. Why shouldn't he have a soothing effect? I was longing for some peace and quiet. Secretly I hoped that from now on the Compsognathus would be busy with the rabbit and would leave me alone, so that I could at least read without being disturbed, and occasionally leave the house without him.

Unfortunately, I was mistaken.

It's true he no longer sat on my newspaper. All day he sat motionless in front of the sofa and waited. But this wasn't the peace and quiet I had hoped for. It was the calm before the storm.

That night I slept badly. I dreamt that a chair fell over and broke to pieces. I dreamt that something was running through the pitch-dark room at an incredible speed. I heard banging. I heard a squeal. Bathed in sweat, I rolled over to the other side. It sounded like all hell was breaking loose.

"Zawinul," I said to myself in the dream, "don't get upset. You're dreaming."

Then I heard the running around again. It went from the bedroom to the living-room, from there to the kitchen, into the corridor, into the bedroom again, into the living-room, and so forth. It was one of those nightmares that doesn't end. I cried out loud and jumped out of the bed.

When I stepped on the broken pieces of a chair in front of my bed, I realized that it wasn't a dream. My chair lay smashed on the floor. The running around stopped. It became very quiet. The dinosaur was squatting in front of the sofa again. The rabbit was nowhere in sight.

"What happened to the rabbit?" I yelled.

"Don't yell like that."

"I'm not yelling!" I yelled.

"You're mean," said the Compsognathus.

"Now you've scared him."

"No, I think it's you who has scared him."

The rabbit was sitting under the sofa, scratching and pretending that all this didn't concern him. He continued to wrinkle his nose.

"Please be so kind," he said, "as to lock up this wild animal. It robs one of one's sleep."

"No!" I yelled.

"What do you mean, Mr. Zawinul?" said the rabbit, wrinkling his nose.

"You see?" yelled the Compsognathus pointing angrily at the rabbit-nose. "The rabbit started it."

"Enough!" I yelled. "I can't stand it anymore. Blue rabbits don't exist. You just made them up!"

"Me?" asked the Compsognathus.

136

"You! And if someone can invent blue rabbits, he can invent much more."

Perhaps, I thought, it was he who had invented Zawinul and not the other way around. And perhaps, I continued to think, he also invented everything I see here.

"Me?" repeated the Compsognathus.

"You."

"Are you trying to say that I made the goldfish up, Zawinul?"

"Yes."

"And the bones in the goldfish too?"

"Yes."

"And are you trying to say that goldfish don't exist, Zawinul?"

"Yes!"

"O? O? O?" said the Compsognathus.

"Gnathus!" I said.

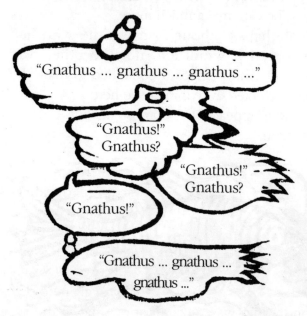

THE END OF ZAWINUL

 That night I had strange dreams. I was crouching in a crevice between two boulders and was excitedly watching a gigantic dragon-fly that was buzzing above me in the sunlight. In the dream I felt the juice dripping from my mouth. When I couldn't bear it anymore, I shot out of my crevice aiming for the dragon fly, opened my mouth wide and—missed it. Furious, I let myself fall on the rock, which hurt so much that I woke up.

I lay on the floor in front of my bed, looked at my legs, and realized to my great joy that I was Zawinul and not a Compsognathus.

"Comps!" I grunted, pulled the blanket down from the bed in order to cover myself, and fell asleep again.

When I looked out of my crevice once again, I saw that the wide land around me was full of tremendous dinosaurs who were peacefully grazing and picking the foliage from the trees. The sun was shining. The dragon-flies from the dream were flying around me, but I didn't feel like eating them anymore. Why not?

"I've got it," I said in the dream. "I'm not a dinosaur at all, I'm Zawinul."

When I woke up, I realized that I was unfortunately mistaken. I was by no means Zawinul. This can't be, I said to myself.

I called my friend because he was the only one I could speak to under these circumstances. After all, he knew roughly what I was talking about. And maybe he could tell me whether I was myself or a dinosaur.

"I haven't heard from you in a long time, Zawinul," he said.

"I don't have time to make phone calls," I said.

"Why not?" asked my friend.

"Zawinul, what are you doing there?" squeaked the Compsognathus at this moment as he tried to take the receiver out of my hand. I was very glad about this, because now I knew that the dinosaur wasn't me, but him.

"I'm using the phone," I said.

The Compsognathus pushed down phone cradle, and the conversation ended.

"Where is the voice now?"

"Gone," I said and dialed again. The Compsognathus waited to hear the voice.

"Is it you, Zawinul?" asked my friend.

"Yes," I said. This call was ended, too, because the Compsognathus pushed the phone cradle down once more.

"Don't let it bother you," he said. "I'm extinct anyway."

I tied him to the bed, because the bed was so heavy that he couldn't pull it through the apartment. I dialed once again.

"How are you?" asked my friend.

"It's unbearable," I said. "It's impossible. Everything's full of goldfish and blue rabbits. And then this dinosaur."

"Compsognathus!" squeaked the Compsognathus.

"Omps!" I whispered.

"What was that?"

"I said, I don't know what to do anymore about this dinosaur."

To make me happy, my friend said, "I found out what 'Compsognathus' means."

"Let me guess," I said. "The wild mouse?"

"No."

"The fast claw?"

"No."

"The little monster?"

142

"No again. It means: the 'elegant jaw.'"

"Very appropriate," I groaned. "And now please tell me what I should do."

"I think you have to put the dinosaur out of your head," said my friend.

"Put him out of my head?" I said. "Can you tell me how to do that?"

"Nothing is easier," said my friend. "You simply think about something else."

"Thanks," I said.

But I couldn't think about anything else. No one can do that. With goldfish it works; if you don't want to think about them, you just think about something else. With blue rabbits it's more difficult. For a long time, I can only think of blue rabbits when I try not to think about them. With the Compsognathus it's impossible to think about anything else. And I had enough. What to do?

"Zawinul," I said to myself, "dinosaurs don't exist. That's certain. All the same, it is difficult to put the dinosaur out of your head. And it's impossible as long as you're called Zawinul. It's no use, you've got to pass this name on."

I asked my friend whether he wanted to be called Zawinul again. He didn't.

Tomorrow I will start looking for a person who wants to be called Zawinul. It's such a beautiful name. It fits women and men. It fits big and small children and all people who want to experience something that is not real. It's hard for me to part with it. Especially now, I think, the name has finally stuck properly. But it has to be. And I am sure that somewhere there is someone who would like to have it.